I'm Going To READ!™

These levels are meant only as guides;
you and your child can best choose a book that's right.

UP TO 50 WORDS

Level 1: Kindergarten–Grade 1 . . . Ages 4–6

- word bank to highlight new words
- consistent placement of text to promote readability
- easy words and phrases
- simple sentences build to make simple stories
- art and design help new readers decode text

UP TO 100 WORDS

Level 2: Grade 1 . . . Ages 6–7

- word bank to highlight new words
- rhyming texts introduced
- more difficult words, but vocabulary is still limited
- longer sentences and longer stories
- designed for easy readability

UP TO 200 WORDS

Level 3: Grade 2 . . . Ages 7–8

- richer vocabulary of up to 200 different words
- varied sentence structure
- high-interest stories with longer plots
- designed to promote independent reading

MORE THAN 300 WORDS

Level 4: Grades 3 and up . . . Ages 8 and up

- richer vocabulary of more than 300 different words
- short chapters, multiple stories, or poems
- more complex plots for the newly independent reader
- emphasis on reading for meaning

LEVEL 2

2 4 6 8 10 9 7 5 3

Published by Sterling Publishing Co., Inc.
387 Park Avenue South, New York, NY 10016
Text © 2007 by Harriet Ziefert Inc.
Illustrations © 2007 by Deborah Zemke
Distributed in Canada by Sterling Publishing
c/o Canadian Manda Group, 165 Dufferin Street,
Toronto, Ontario, Canada M6K 3H6
Distributed in the United Kingdom by GMC Distribution Services,
Castle Place, 166 High Street, Lewes, East Sussex, England BN7 1XU
Distributed in Australia by Capricorn Link (Australia) Pty. Ltd.
P.O. Box 704, Windsor, NSW 2756, Australia

I'm Going To Read is a trademark of Sterling Publishing Co., Inc.

Library of Congress Cataloging-in-Publication Data

Zemke, Deborah.
Green boots, blue hair, polka-dot underwear /
pictures by Deborah Zemke.
    p. cm.—(I'm going to read)
Summary: Easy-to-read text invites the reader to choose
what to wear, from hats in assorted colors to different kinds
of sleepwear.
ISBN-13: 978-1-4027-4245-3
ISBN-10: 1-4027-4245-2
[1. Clothing and dress—Fiction. 2. Choice—Fiction.] I. Title.

PZ7.Z423Pur 2007
[E]—dc22

                                        2006022630

Printed in China

Sterling ISBN-13: 978-1-4027-4245-3
ISBN-10: 1-4027-4245-2

For information about custom editions, special sales, premium and
corporate purchases, please contact Sterling Special Sales
Department at 800-805-5489 or specialsales@sterlingpub.com.

GREEN BOOTS

BLUE HAIR

POLKA-DOT UNDERWEAR

Pictures by Deborah Zemke

Sterling Publishing Co., Inc.
New York

CHAPTER 1

YOU
CHOOSE

WHAT WOULD YOU LIKE TO WEAR?

blue hat

red hat

crown

green hat

WHAT WOULD YOU LIKE TO HAVE?

blue hair

brown hair

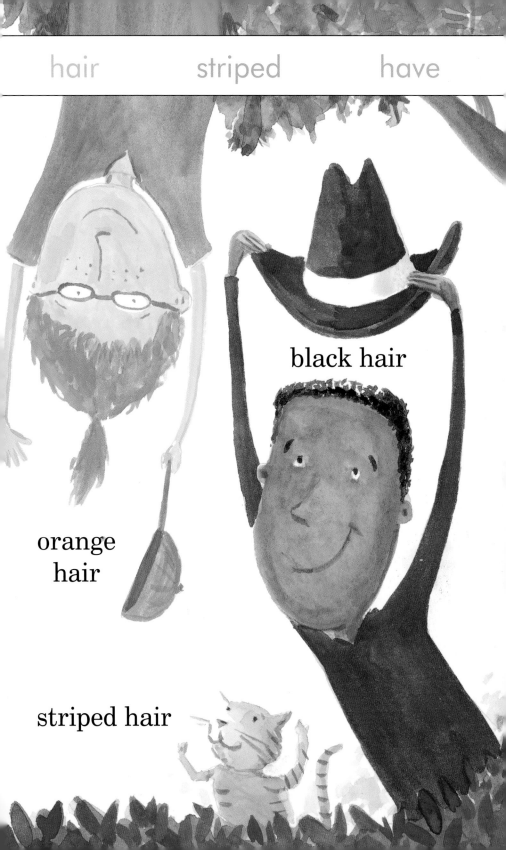

black hair

orange hair

striped hair

sparkles

dots

WHAT WOULD YOU LIKE TO WEAR?

jeans

shorts

pants   skirt

WHAT WOULD YOU LIKE TO WEAR?

high socks

low socks

striped socks

no socks

cowboy boots

sneakers

WHAT WOULD YOU LIKE TO WEAR?

slippers

rain boots

You choose!

WHATEVER!

CHAPTER 2

CHOOSE AGAIN

WHAT WOULD YOU LIKE TO WEAR TO SCHOOL?

stars

stripes

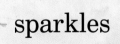

sparkles

dots

WHAT WOULD YOU LIKE TO WEAR TO GO SWIMMING?

sunglasses

swim mask

shark suit

swimsuit

red gloves

blue gloves

WHAT WOULD
YOU LIKE
TO WEAR TO PLAY
IN THE SNOW?

green gloves

baseball glove

WHAT WOULD YOU LIKE TO WEAR TO A COSTUME PARTY?

red nose

brown ears

green
teeth

striped
tail

WHAT WOULD YOU LIKE TO WEAR TO BED?

pajamas

slippers

nightgown

polka-dot
underwear

WHAT WOULD YOU LIKE TO WEAR IN YOUR DREAMS?

You choose!

WHAT WILL YOU WEAR TODAY?